This book belongs to:

_____

To the great teachers.

Thank you!

www.plantlovegrow.com

©plantlovegrow 2013
©Elaheh Bos 2013

ISBN: 978-1493737864
ISBN: 1493737864

Special thanks to
Isabelle Lefebvre, Soraya Tohidi & Sabine Yimlim
for their advice, experience and encouragement.

Dear parents,

This book was created as a fun introduction to simple techniques of anxiety management.

It is also a tool to help young children get ready for school.

You will be the guide in this process, helping your children connect the examples in the book to what they are experiencing individually.

They will have plenty of opportunities to learn their alphabet, numbers, colors, and shapes. The goal here is to get them excited at the possibility of what awaits them and to help them feel prepared for the uncertainties of change.

Best of luck on your journey.

Maya, the brave!

I am ready for school!

By
Elaheh Bos

Ever since Maya found out
she would be starting school,
she couldn't sleep.

Her eyes wouldn't close,
not even a little.

She tried
looking for monsters
to pass the time,
but there
weren't any.

She tried counting
the stars on her pajamas,
but there were
too many.

She tried
telling a story to Crock,
but Crock
wasn't paying attention.

Too many

questions and worries

hopped around in Maya's mind,
making far too much noise
for Maya to rest.

What if there is no playtime?
What if there is no snack time?
Will I make friends?
What if I don't know what to do?
What if there is no washroom?
What if I don't understand what they say?
What if I cannot find my favorite socks?
Will I be able to bring my toys with me?
What if I don't know anyone there?
What if school is boring?
Will the teacher like me?
What if school is too hard?
Will I have fun?

Eventually,
Maya fell asleep.

not because the questions
and worries went away,
but because Koala
wouldn't sleep
unless Maya
tried to sleep as well.

The next day,
Maya read a book about a brave knight
who went on many different quests.

Maya loved stories of adventures and quests,
of people being brave
and accomplishing great things.

She wanted to be brave
just like the knight.

The first brave thing Maya did
was tell her mother
about the worries
and questions
that followed her around.

Together, they talked.

They made a plan to help Maya
feel prepared for school.

Maya was now ready to be brave and have fun.
She was ready to face dragons,
look for answers, and go on all the quests
so that she could become a brave knight.

You're starting school soon too, aren't you?

Why don't you join Maya on her journey?

Will you please
help me
on my quests?

After she completes each quest,
Maya will collect a badge.

You don't have to complete
all the quests all at one time.

Try to do as many as you can
alongside Maya before you start school.

Quest 1

I, _____

pledge to always
do my best,
to share my fears,
and to try
to have lots of fun
on this journey.

I am brave!

I am awesome!

I am amazing!

Before starting any journey,
brave knights make a pledge.

They say special words out loud
to give them strength and energy.

Help Maya by repeating the pledge
along with her.

A pledge is a promise.
Write your name and say
the following words out loud:

Super!

Now that you have completed this quest,
find the badge for it at the end of the book.
Cut it out and glue it here.

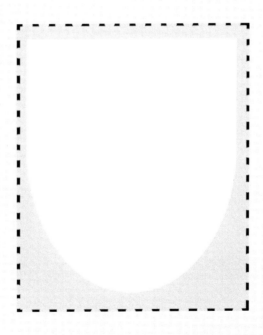

Pledge badge

Quest 2

Everyone has worries and questions, even brave knights.
It's good to let these worries out so they don't take
too much place in our minds and hearts.

For this quest, find a small box.
This is now your worry box.
Draw three things that worry you about starting school.
Place these pictures in the box.

By putting them in the box,
you take the worries out of your mind.

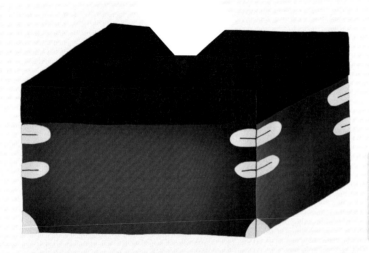

An adult can take the worries
out of the box when you feel
they are no longer heavy
on your heart.

Fantastic!

Now that you have completed this quest,
find the badge for it at the end of the book.
Cut it out and glue it here.

Worry box badge

 # Quest 3

All knights like to draw maps
and plan where they are going.
Here's your chance to do the same.

If you can, take a photo of your future classroom or school
and glue it in the square below. If not, use your amazing drawing talents,
and draw a picture of a classroom.
You may have to use your wonderful imagination!

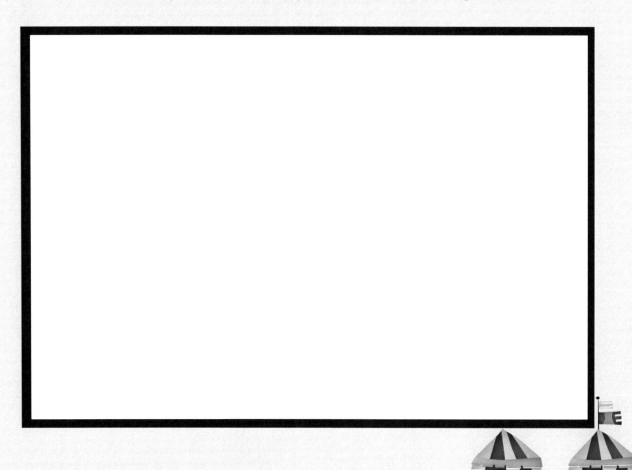

Tremendous!

Now that you have completed this quest,
find the badge for it at the end of the book.
Cut it out and glue it here.

Visualization badge

Quest 4

All knights have qualities.
Some knights are brave.
Some knights are kind and like to help others.
Some knights are artistic and creative.
These strengths helps knights keep going on their journey.
Circle as many qualities about yourself as you can find.

I am cheerful

I am responsible

I am honest

I am patient

I care

I smile a lot

I am kind

I am artistic

I am helpful

I share well

Awesome!

I am polite

Now that you have completed this quest,
find the badge for it at the end of the book.
Cut it out and glue it here.

I am generous

I play well
with others

My qualities badge

Quest 5

Maya was worried that she wouldn't make new friends at school.
It's okay to worry about things like that,
but Maya forgot that she is kind, likes to share,
plays well and creates amazing adventures.
Who wouldn't want to be her friend?

Just like Maya, you have many great qualities.
Remember all the ones you discovered about yourself on Quest 4?
You will be a wonderful friend too!
Now draw yourself playing with a new friend you may meet at school.

Beautiful!

Now that you have completed this quest,
find the badge for it at the end of the book.
Cut it out and glue it here.

Making a friend badge

Quest 6

All knights practice to become good at things
such as riding horses and looking for frogs under bridges.
Maya needs help practicing cutting, coloring, and gluing.
She needs help with tracing, too.

Here, please help her trace all the shapes and patterns.

Take your time and do your best.
Ask for help if you need it.
Try to name the shapes as you trace them.

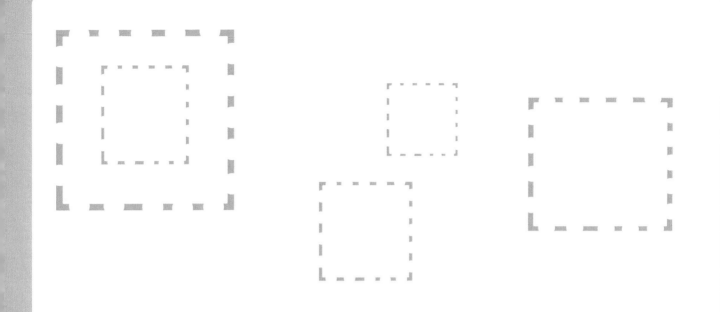

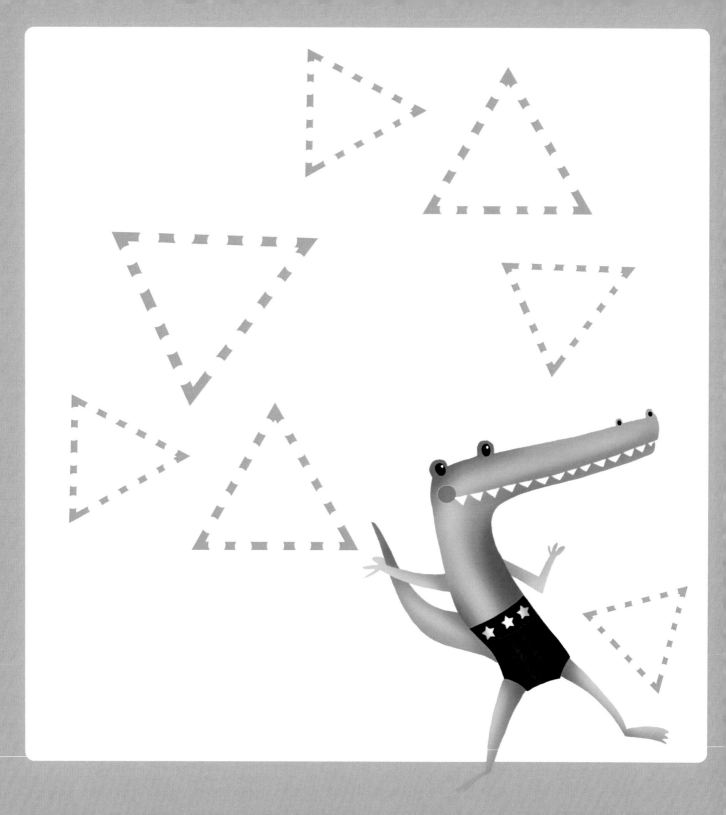

Fantastic!

Now that you have completed this quest,
find the badge for it at the end of the book.
Cut it out and glue it here.

Tracing shapes badge

Quest 7

Help Maya learn her colors.
Use markers or crayons to fill in each diamond with a different color.
Get some help if you need with naming the colors.

Colorful!

Now that you have completed this quest,
find the badge for it at the end of the book.
Cut it out and glue it here.

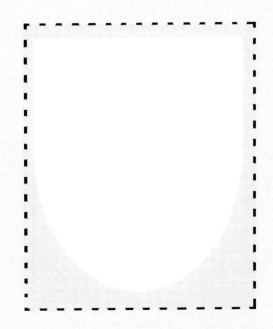

Color power badge

Quest 8

All knights need to listen well because it helps them
to understand what they are being told.
This is also a good skill to learn for school.
Can you help Maya by listening to three different stories at home?

You must be very quiet and listen during the stories to get this skill right.
You can also ask questions about the story to show that you were listening well.

Story 1 - I was as quiet as a mouse.

Story 2 - I was as quiet as a sleeping squirrel.

Story 3 - I was as quiet as a turtle.

Peaceful!

Now that you have completed this quest,
find the badge for it at the end of the book.
Cut it out and glue it here.

Listening skills badge

 # Quest 9

All knights know about themselves. Knowing their names and which castle they live in can be useful should they ever meet a friendly wizard. Answer these questions about yourself.

When you are finished, draw a picture of yourself as a knight.

Get as much help as you need to answer these questions.

My name: _____

My age: _____

How old I will be when I start school:
_____

My phone number:
_____

The name of my school:
_____

What I like to eat:
_____

What I like to do to have fun:
_____
_____
_____
_____

Brilliant!

Now that you have completed this quest,
find the badge for it at the end of the book.
Cut it out and glue it here.

About me badge

Quest 10

All knights know how important it is to try something before doing it for real.
It makes them feel prepared, more relaxed, and happier
when they get a chance to practice something new.
Show Maya how to do this. Imagine that you are already at your new school.

With a loud and clear voice, practice the following:

Ask for help after you scrape your knee. ☐

Ask to go to the washroom. ☐

Ask a new friend to play with you. ☐

Now try this.
Choose something that worries you
and practice doing it or saying it. ☐

How brave!

Now that you have completed this quest,
find the badge for it at the end of the book.
Cut it out and glue it here.

Practice is awesome badge

Quest 11

Sometimes, even knights feel a little nervous when they visit a new castle.

Just like you and Maya, they can't always bring
their favorite toy or Koala to keep them company.
However they might carry a special memory in their heart or in their pockets.
This makes them feel safe until they realize they have nothing to worry about.

To complete this quest, think of something special you can carry in your heart
when you go to school, and make a drawing of it.
Or find a small photo that makes you feel happy.

Keep it somewhere special.
You'll know where to find it
if you decide to take it with you
when you begin school.

Heartfelt!

Now that you have completed this quest,
find the badge for it at the end of the book.
Cut it out and glue it here.

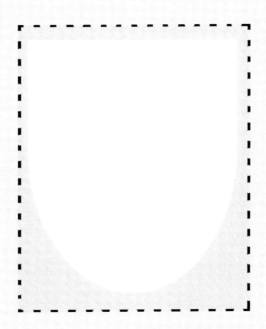

Holding on to a memory badge

Quest 12

Knights need to know how to cut and glue shapes to decorate their shields.
These are skills you will also learn at your new school.
Maybe you can help Maya by practicing with her. Get some help if you need it!

Cut different shapes out of paper.
Try naming them as you glue them on the next few pages.

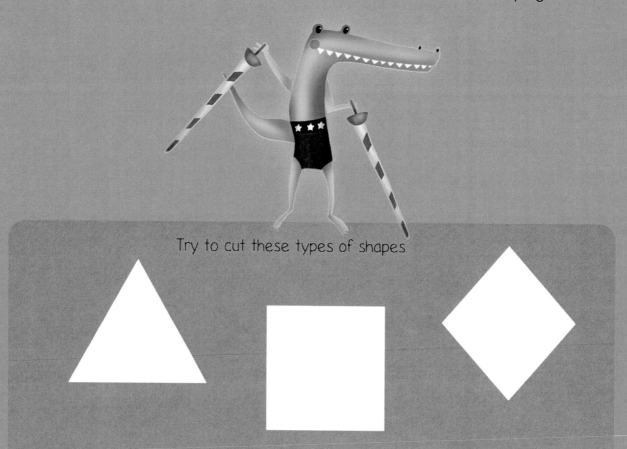

Try to cut these types of shapes.

Glue your shapes here

Glue your shapes here

Snip, snap, awesome!

Now that you have completed this quest,
find the badge for it at the end of the book.
Cut it out and glue it here.

Cutting & gluing skills badge

Quest 13

Time to practice your focusing muscles! focusing is a useful skill
that can help you keep your eyes on your goal.
Knights focus when they need to do activities that require lots of attention,
like dragon taming and target practice.
Help Maya learn to focus by doing these fun games with her.

Game 1: Add the correct colors to these patterns.

Game 2 - Match the shadow with the image.

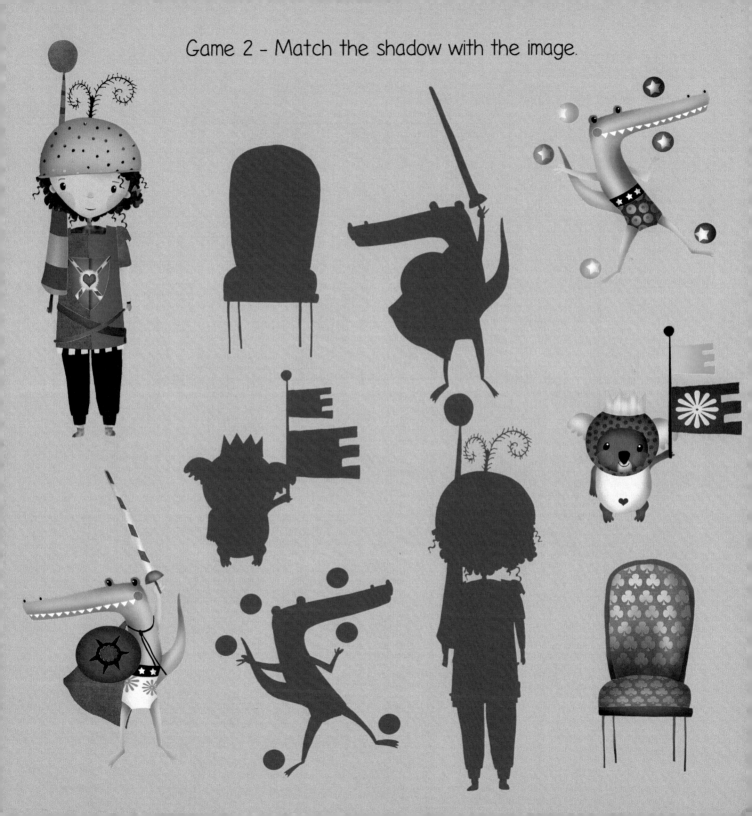

Game 3 - Find the three differences in the pictures.

Astounding!

Now that you have completed this quest,
find the badge for it at the end of the book.
Cut it out and glue it here.

Focusing muscles badge

Quest 14

Knights learn to count so they can get the arrows they need
for the three arrow competition or figure out how many carrots
to feed their horses. Show Maya how you can count
by matching the objects to the correct numbers.

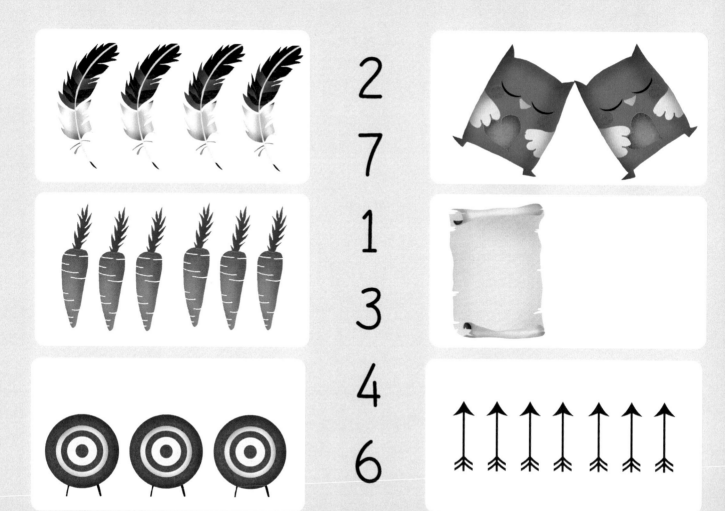

2

7

1

3

4

6

Wonderful!

Now that you have completed this quest,
find the badge for it at the end of the book.
Cut it out and glue it here.

Number magic badge

Quest 15

Sometimes, even brave knights get worried, afraid, or angry.
Their hearts start to beat really quickly. They feel really hot.
If they are angry, they might feel like they are dragons breathing fire.
It can seem very loud in their head, as if everyone is talking at the same time.
When this happens, knights know to use their special breathing.

They breath in and out very slowly.
As they breathe in, they imagine themselves calm and relaxed.
As they breathe out, they imagine themselves feeling better.
After a few more breaths, they can also try to imagine themselves
being able to talk about what made them feel worried, afraid or angry.

Close your eyes and practice breathing like a knight.
Take some long slow breaths in and out.

I practiced once. ☐

I practiced twice. ☐

I practiced three times. ☐

Relaxing!

Now that you have completed this quest,
find the badge for it at the end of the book.
Cut it out and glue it here.

Breathing like a knight badge

Congratulations!

You did it!

Wow! Congratulations! You did it!
You have just helped Maya complete all her quests.
Just like you, she is now ready for school.
Maya was worried when she started this journey,
but now she feels more relaxed.
She knows that no matter what comes her way,
she will be able to face it like a brave knight.

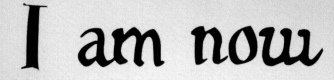

I am now
_____,

the brave!

Extra challenges

Eating habits challenge

Knights need to eat healthy foods
so they can be strong
and have lots of energy.
Maya likes all kinds of fruits and vegetables.
She is ready to try a few more.
Help Maya get ready for school
by completing this quest with her.

Try the following:

a green vegetable   a round vegetable
a new vegetable   a red fruit
a yellow fruit   an orange fruit
a new juice   a new meal
a new kind of soup

Draw a picture of yourself
eating your snack
or lunch at your new school.

Dress myself challenge

All knights must be able
to get dressed by themselves.
Sometimes, they have squires
or assistants to help them a little,
but when they go to new places,
they have to be able to do it
on their own.
Help Maya with this challenge
by doing the following:

I can put on my underwear by myself.
I can put on my shirt by myself.
I can put on my pants by myself.
I can put on my socks by myself.
I can put on my shoes by myself.
I can tie my shoes by myself.
I can put on my jacket by myself.
I can zip/fasten my jacket by myself.
I can put on my hat by myself.

Draw a picture of yourself
all dressed up.

Badges

Cut on the
indicated line.

Do not rip
the pages
because
that might
weaken
the book.

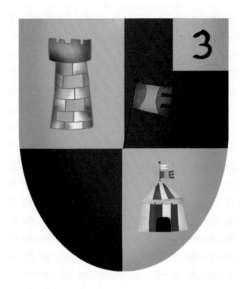

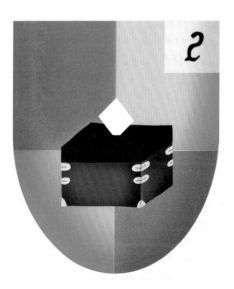

Badges

Cut on the indicated line.

Do not rip the pages because that might weaken the book.

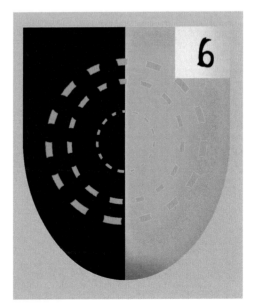

Badges

Cut on the indicated line.

Do not rip the pages because that might weaken the book.

Badges

Cut on the
indicated line.

Do not rip
the pages
because
that might
weaken
the book.

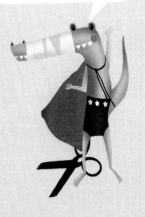

Don't juggle with scissors,
and good luck at school!
I'm proud of you!

15

13

14

plant
love
grow

CPSIA information can be obtained
at www.ICGtesting.com
Printed in the USA
BVXC01n1945290317
479791BV00005B/29